D1472565

FREDERICK WARNE
An Imprint of Penguin Random House LLC, New York

Penguin supports copyright. Copyright fuels creativity, encourages diverse voices,
promotes free speech, and creates a vibrant culture. Thank you for buying an
authorized edition of this book and for complying with copyright laws by
not reproducing, scanning, or distributing any part of it in any form
without permission. You are supporting writers and allowing Penguin to
continue to publish books for every reader.

Copyright © Frederick Warne & Co. Ltd, 2021
Peter Rabbit™ & Beatrix Potter™ Frederick Warne & Co.
Frederick Warne & Co. is the owner of all rights, copyrights, and
trademarks in the Beatrix Potter character names and illustrations

Published in 2021 by Frederick Warne,
an imprint of Penguin Random House LLC, New York.
Manufactured in China.

Visit us online at www.penguinrandomhouse.com.

ISBN: 9780241473146

001

PETER RABBIT™

I LOVE YOU GRANDPA

When
THE DAY
begins
AND

There's
LOTS
TO DO,

I can't WAIT to share

adventures WITH YOU.

You
TEACH
ME

ALL *about* THE
WORLD *you* KNOW,

so I can find MY own

WAY

as I
learn
AND
GROW.

I am
NEVER
afraid

TO *Try*
SOMETHING
NEW

BECAUSE
you
BELIEVE
IN *me*

AND ALL
that
I DO.

I AM feeling SAD,

and YOUR
GIANT
hugs

As THE
BRIGHT
sun
sets

on
OUR day
OF
FUN,

I am
PROUD
to BE
called

your
LITTLE
one.

GRANDPA,
your
LOVE
makes
ME *feel*

BOLD
and
STRONG,

and
I know
THAT
by **YOUR**
SIDE *is*